Why am I Here?

This book was made possible in part by The Marge and Charles J. Schott Foundation

Why am I Here?

a story about becoming the-best-version-of-yourself!

MATTHEW KELLY
with illustrations by hazel mitchell

The boy's name was Max.

He was just old enough to start
thinking about life's big questions.

On weekends Max's Grandpa often took him fishing.
Max liked being on the lake. It was quiet and peaceful.

But most of all Max loved spending time
with his Grandpa.

One Saturday, they arrived at the lake, threw their lines into the water, and waited. They talked for a while about school and baseball, and then Max asked, "Grandpa, can I ask you a question?"

"Fire away, Kiddo," Grandpa replied.
"Why am I here ... in this world?" Max inquired.

"To go fishing,"
his Grandpa said with a big smile.

"No, Grandpa," Max chuckled, as he cast his line again.
"Seriously, what is life really all about?
Why am I here?"

Grandpa smiled his all knowing smile.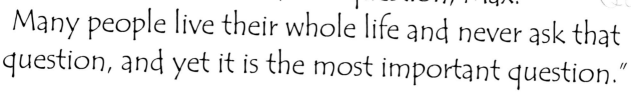
"What a wonderful question, Max.
Many people live their whole life and never ask that
question, and yet it is the most important question."

Max sat listening carefully to what his
Grandpa was saying. "To help us both to understand
your question, Max, let me ask you a few questions."
"Fire away," Max giggled.
"What do you know about birds?" Grandpa asked.
"They have wings," Max replied, "and they fly."
"Very good, but do they bark?"
"No Grandpa, don't be silly!
Birds don't bark. Dogs bark!" Max said.

"Excellent. Now, tell me, what are birds good at being?"
"Birds are good at being birds ... right?" Max responded,
a little unsure of himself.

"Exactly!" Grandpa continued,
"A bird doesn't try to be a fish
or a lion,

it just enjoys being the best bird it can be!"

"Okay Max, I have another one for you.
What is a fish good at being?"
"A fish is good at being a fish!"
Max exclaimed with much more confidence.

"Exactly. A fish doesn't try to be a bird or
an elephant, it just tries to be the best fish it
can be in every moment of every day."

"But what does all this have to do with me, Grandpa?"

"Well, Max, if a fish is good a being a fish,
and a bird is good a being a bird, then you Max,
are good at being Max. You are not here to be Michael
or Hannah or Will, you are here to be you."

"I guess it would be pretty boring if
we were all the same, Grandpa."
"That's exactly right Max, and we are happiest when
we are being ourselves. Imagine how unhappy a bird
would be if it spent it's whole life trying to be a fish.
It wouldn't matter how hard that bird tried,
it would never be good at being a fish.
A bird will always fail when it tries to be a fish.

Imagine how miserable an elephant would be if
it tried to be a giraffe. An elephant will
always fail when it tries to be a giraffe.
And you and I, Max, we will always fail
if we try to be someone other than who we are."
Grandpa continued,
"Now, getting back to your question. Why are you here?
You are here to become the-best-version-of-yourself!"

As they sat fishing quietly, Max thought to himself,
"I am here to be the best Max I can be!"

After Max had some time to think about all this, Grandpa continued, "Sometimes Max, we do things that help us become the-best-version-of-ourselves, and sometimes we do things that don't.

This week I want you to pay close attention to the choices you make. Now that we have had this conversation, you'll start to notice moments every day when you have to make a choice, and hopefully you will start making the choices that help you to become the-best-version-of-yourself!"

"Max, if you're ever confused about whether or not you should do something, just ask yourself, 'Will this help me to become the-best-version-of-myself?'"

"Now, why are you here?" Grandpa quizzed Max.
"To become the-best-version-of-myself!"
he answered with a smile. It made sense to him.
Grandpa put another worm on his line
and threw it back into the water.

At that very moment, Max felt a tug on his line.

On Monday morning when Max was helping his mother pack his lunch, he wanted to fill his lunchbox with candy and potato chips, but he remembered the conversation with his Grandpa, and wondered to himself, "What can I eat that will help me become the-best-version-of-myself?"

Max really wanted the candy and potato chips, but he knew an apple and a sandwich would help to make him the-best-version-of-himself. So, Max decided to have an apple and a sandwich for lunch.

At school Max's teacher, Miss Lauren, asked the class what they had done over the weekend. Max raised his hand and when she called on him, he stood up and said,

"I went fishing with my Grandpa and learned about why I am here."

"Why are you here, Max?" his teacher asked.

"To become the-best-version-of-myself!" Max replied.

"What a wonderful discovery!" Miss Lauren exclaimed
as she turned to write,
BECOME THE-BEST-VERSION-OF-YOURSELF
across the top of the chalkboard.

After lunch, during art class, Jimmy
took Max's markers. Miss Lauren asked,
"Jimmmy, are you being the-best-version-of-yourself?"
Jimmy looked at Miss Lauren sheepishly,
then turned to Max, gave back his markers,
and apologized.

After school, Max didn't feel like doing his homework.
He really wanted to watch TV, but as he sat down
and reached for the remote he thought to himself,
"Which will help me become
the-best-version-of-myself,
doing my homework or watching TV?"

Max decided to do his homework.
It was difficult to focus,
but when he was finished, he felt good.

The next morning,
the first thing Miss Lauren did was ask the class,

"Why are you here?"

Ellie raised her hand,
and when she was called on, said,
"To become the-best-version-of-myself!"

Miss Lauren asked Jake next and he replied,
"To become the-best-version-of-myself!"

Then Miss Lauren asked the whole class,
and they cried out together,
"To become the-best-version-of-myself!"
"Fantastic!" Miss Lauren applauded them.
"Let's make sure to remember that throughout the day."

Then she asked the students to give examples of how they were becoming the-best-version-of-themselves. Hands shot up all over the classroom.
Max's classmates were excited to share about how they were becoming the-best-version-of-themselves.

After school on Tuesday,
Max went shopping with his mother.
He saw a new video game at the store
and asked his mother if he could have it.

Max's mother looked at it and said,
"It seems very violent Max. Remember your
conversation with Grandpa? Do you think it will help
you become the-best-version-of-yourself?"

Max realized that even though all his friends had the new video game, maybe it wasn't the best choice for him. He really wanted the video game, but he wanted to be the best-version-of-himself even more.

"You're right Mom," he said
as he put the video game back on the shelf.

When they got home Max's dad was sitting on the couch, watching football and eating an enormous bag of potato chips.

"Is that helping you become
the-best-version-of-yourself, Dad?" Max asked,
and giggled as he grabbed his helmet
and went outside to ride his bike with his friends.

At school on Friday, Max was tired of waiting
in line at the drinking fountain and pushed Hannah
to get to the front of the line.
Miss Lauren saw him do this and asked,
"Max, was that the-best-version-of-yourself?"

"No, Miss Lauren," Max replied. Then turning
to Hannah he helped her pick up her things, and said,
"I'm sorry for pushing you Hannah.
That was selfish and mean of me. I won't do it again."

After school, Max was thirsty. He felt like a cola,
but he thought to himself,
"Water is better for me. It will help me
become the-best-version-of-myself."

So he drank a big glass of cold water.

It was refreshing
and filled Max with energy.

After dinner, Max cleared the table with his mother and then helped his little sister put her toys away.

While he was doing it
he came to a wonderful realization...

"Whenever I do the things that help me
become the-best-version-of-myself
I feel really good inside. I guess Grandpa was right!
I am happiest when I am trying to
be the best Max I can be."

As Max climbed into bed that night,
he made a list in his mind of all the things
he had said and done that helped him
become the-best-version-of-himself....

I thanked my Mom for making me breakfast…
worked hard in school…
ate healthy food…

tried my best at baseball practice
(when I felt like being lazy)…
drank plenty of water…

did my chores without being asked…
helped my little sister put her toys away…

Max felt proud and joyful about this list.

Then Max made a list of the things he
had said and done that day that didn't
help him become the-best-version-of-himself...

I talked to Jamal in class
while Miss Lauren was speaking…
pushed Hannah on the playground…
ate too many cookies…
and told a lie to my parents…

As he thought about this list, Max felt disappointed
in himself. He didn't like feeling this way,
so he decided he would try harder the next day.
He also decided that from that night on, he would
think about his day each night before he went to sleep.

Max drifted off to sleep
with a smile on his face thinking,
"I am not perfect, but I am better today
than I was yesterday and every day,
in every way, I am working on becoming
the-best-version-of-myself!"

The End

Max's Bookshop

Visit www.MaxsBookshop.com to learn more.

About the Author

Matthew Kelly is an internationally renowned speaker and *New York Times* bestselling author of more than a dozen books including: *The Rhythm of Life, The Seven Levels of Intimacy, Building Better Families, and The Dream Manager.*
Kelly has dedicated his entire adult life to encouraging people of all ages to live with passion and purpose by striving to become the-best-version-of-themselves. *Why am I Here?* is his first children's book.

About the Illustrator

Hazel Mitchell has drawn since she can remember. She loves to illustrate for children and has worked on several books. Her studio is in Maine; originally she is from Yorkshire, England. Mitchell has clients worldwide and her work has been received by the British Royal Family. See more of her work at www.hazelmitchell.com

This book was made possible in part by
The Marge and Charles J. Schott Foundation

First Edition 2010
Library of Congress
Catalog-in-Publication Data is available.
Library of Congress Control Number: 2009910142

ISBN-10 0-9841318-0-9
ISBN13 978-0-9841318-0-8
2 4 6 8 10 9 7 5 3 1
Printed in Mexico
This book was hand illustrated in watercolor and ink
by Hazel Mitchell

Beacon Publishing
West Palm Beach Florida 33404
United States of America

www.theBestVersionofYourself.com